Christmas tree — A truck with many extra clearance lights

Crate of sand — A cargo of sugar

Dig out — To make a fast start

Dog catcher — Any rig fast enough to catch up to and pass a Greyhound bus

Double nickels — The 55-mile-an-hour speed limit

Dusting — Driving on the shoulder of the road

Fender bender — An accident

Going home gear — The highest gear

Granny gear — The lowest gear

Greasy side up — Overturned vehicle

Green stamps — Speeding tickets

Handle — A C.B. operator's nickname

Harvey wallbanger — A reckless driver

Hood-lifter — A mechanic in a truck stop

FRANK AND ERNEST ON THE ROAD

FRANK AND ERNEST ON THE ROAD

By Alexandra Day

SCHOLASTIC
HARDCOVER

SCHOLASTIC INC. · New York

Thanks to Tom Dalzell for his keen interest,
and his excellent contributions to
Frank and Ernest's trucking vocabulary
—AD

Library of Congress Cataloging-in-Publication Data

Day, Alexandra.
Frank and Ernest : on the road / written and illustrated by Alexandra Day.
p. cm.
Summary: While making a delivery for a friend,
an elephant and a bear become familiar with the experiences and language
of truck drivers. Includes a brief glossary of CB slang.
ISBN 0-590-45048-4
[1. Elephants — Fiction. 2. Bears — Fiction. 3. Citizen band
radio — Slang — Fiction. 4. Truck drivers — Fiction.] I. Title.
PZ7.D32915Frn 1992
[E] — dc20   91-30383
CIP
AC

12 11 10 9 8 7 6 5 4 3 2 1   4 5 6 7 8 9/9
Printed in the U.S.A.   36
First Scholastic printing, February 1994

Alexandra Day's art
was done in oil and watercolor.

"I'll bet they can help me do the job."

"Hi, Frank. Good to meet you, Ernest. My name is Steve. I'll only be away three days, but my truck has an important fruit delivery to make. I hope you guys can handle it. Just remember to smile and comb your hair."

"Don't worry, Steve, we can do the job."

"Frank, I never knew how many different languages there were for different businesses. We need to learn truck language if we're going to do a good job."

"Hi, fellas. My name is Janet Parker. This is your
base station. I'm right here at the other end
of this CB radio if you two need any advice.
I hope Steve knew what he was doing
when he hired you two cradle babies.
Here are your flying orders. Keep
in touch."

"It's beautiful, Ernest. I've always wanted to drive
a big truck."

"Me too, Frank. Let's take turns."

"Whoever rides shotgun will look up all the words we need in this book."

"I've just found out what Steve meant by telling us to 'remember to smile and comb your hair.' "

"And here's what Janet meant by base station, cradle babies, and flying orders."

Rides shotgun — the trucker's helper who rides in the passenger seat; named for shotgun carrier who sat next to the stagecoach driver

Smile and comb your hair — drive carefully and don't get a ticket

Base station — the CB transmitter at a truck's headquarters

Cradle babies — a new trucker, or a shy CB operator

Flying orders — instructions for the trip

"Let's help the dock walloper load the truck."

"Now our truck is just a load of holes, but we'll soon change that."

Dock walloper — the cargo loader

Load of holes — an empty truck

"You drive first."

"It's very comfortable in this seat. Let's figure out
how to use our CB radio."

"The book says that CB stands for citizen band."

"Truckers have made up a language they use when they talk on their CB's. They use it for talking to other truckers or to their base station."

"I saw our fishing poles on top of the truck."

"Here's the lollipop."

"I'll keep reading and we'll learn all we need to know."

Fishing pole — antenna

Lollipop — microphone

"Here I am behind the roulette wheel. I'm releasing the Emma Jesse brake."

"We're driving out onto the concrete slab, and we'll follow the banana peel to our destination."

Roulette wheel — the steering wheel

Emma Jesse brake — the emergency brake

Concrete slab — the highway

Banana peel — the yellow stripe running down the middle of a road

"Breaker, breaker. This is Frank and Ernest on channel 19. How do we make the trip?"

"I hear you, good buddy. You're coming in wall to wall and treetop tall."

"When are we supposed to call you, Janet?"

"Just when you have trouble, or see something unusual."

"Let the channels roll."

Breaker, breaker — a request to break in and talk

Make the trip — "How well are you receiving my signal?"

Good buddy — a friendly name for any fellow CB operator

Wall to wall and treetop tall — receiving a strong CB signal

Let the channels roll — let others talk

"This is Frank calling."

"Furry Face is fine, what's your handle?"

"You need a handle, Frank. There are a thousand Franks out there. How do you like Furry Face?"

"Bird."

"Well, what is it like in the front yard?"

"I see a portable floor with a load of sticks,

a muck truck,

a thermos bottle,

 a big dog,

a kiddie car,

 a draggin' wagon,

a rolling bear,

and the road
is a licorice stick."

"Ernest, let's stop at this oasis and put on the feed bags. This looks like a good bean store."

"I would like a cup of road tar."

Oasis — a truck stop

Put on the feed bags — to eat

Bean store — a roadside restaurant

Road tar — coffee

"Bird, this is Furry Face's partner. Can you give me a handle?"

"How do you like Nose?"

"Nose is fine. I just wanted to tell you it's cats and dogs."

"Well, Nose, just tell Furry Face to cool it, put on the air, and dead pedal."

"Okay, Bird, I just hope this doesn't turn into dandruff, or even confetti."

"Ten-four, Nose!"

Cats and dogs — a very heavy rain

Cool it — slow down

Put on the air — apply the brakes

Dead pedal — drive slowly

Dandruff — a light snowfall

Confetti — a heavy snowfall

Ten-four — your message is received

"I'm glad the window washer is gone."

"Look at that outdoor TV. I wish we could stop and see the movie."

"Watch out, there's a padiddle!"

"That one nearly blew our doors off!"

"I hope a bear on rubber pulls him over before he buys the farm."

Window washer—a rain shower

Outdoor TV—a drive-in theater

Padiddle—a car with only one working headlight

Blew the doors off—occurs when one vehicle passes another very rapidly

Bear on rubber—a police car

Buys the farm—to get killed in an accident

"I'm checking my eyes for pinholes. Let's make a pit stop."

"Good idea, Ernest. I think our ship is sinking, so let's fill it with motion lotion."

"Looks as though we'll just make it in time."

Checking my eyes for pinholes — getting sleepy

Pit stop — a visit to a gas station

Our ship is sinking — our truck is running out of gas

Motion lotion — gasoline or diesel fuel

"I'm glad the yardbird is taking over. It's hard to park the truck and spot the body."

Yardbird — a truck handler

Spot the body — detach the trailer (cargo holder) from the tractor (the driving portion)

"Welcome back, Furry Face and Nose! I hear you ran into some deep water, but came through it like BTO's."

"We tried hard, Steve, and we had fun. I hope we can drive again."

"You're real gear jammers, and I sure do thank you."

"Starve the bears, Steve."

Deep water — a flooded road

BTO's — big time operators

Gear jammers — professional truckers

Starve the bears — don't get a ticket

"Let me get your picture
in front of my rig."

Rig—a tractor-trailer unit, or the tractor by itself